D1096153

Well,

when that heard her,

that gave an awful shriek

and away that flew into the dark,

# AND SHE NEVER SAW IT ANY MORE.

YOUR NAME'S TOM TIT TOT.

Next day that there little thing looked

so maliceful when he came for the flax.

And when night came she heard that knocking

against the windowpanes. She oped the window,

and that come right in on the ledge. That

was grinning from ear to ear, and oo that's

tail was twirling round so fast.

"What's my name?" that says,

as that gave her the skeins.

"Is that Solomon?" she says,

pretending to be afeard.

"Noo, 't ain't," that says,

and that came further into the room.

"Well, is that Zebedee?" says she again.

"Noo, 't ain't," says the impet.

And then that laughed and twirled that's tail

till you couldn't hardly see it.

"Take time, woman," that says. "Next guess,

and you're mine." And that stretched out

that's black hands at her.

Well, she backed a step or two, and she

looked at it, and then she laughed out,

and says she, pointing her finger at it:

# NIMMY NIMMY NOT

Well, he hadn't eaten but a mouthful or so,

when he stops and begins to laugh.

"What is it?" says she.

"A-why," says he, "I was out a-hunting today,

and I got away to a place in the wood I'd

never seen before. And there was an old

chalk pit. And I heard a kind of a sort of

humming. So I got off my hobby, and I went

right quiet to the pit, and I looked down.

Well, what should there be but the funniest

little black thing you ever set eyes on. And

what was that doing, but that had a little

spinning wheel, and that was spinning

wonderful fast, and twirling that's tail.

And as that span that sang:

# NIMMY NIMMY NOT
# MY NAME'S TOM TIT TOT.

Well, when the girl heard this,
she felt as if she could have
jumped out of her skin for joy,
but she didn't say a word.

At last it came to the last day but one.
The impet came at night along with the
five skeins, and that said, "What, ain't
you got my name yet?"

"Is that Nicodemus?" says she.

"Noo, 't ain't," that says.

"Is that Sammle?" says she.

"Noo, 't ain't," that says.

"A-well, is that Methusalem?" says she.

"Noo, 't ain't that neither," that says.

Then that looks at her with that's eyes
like a coal o' fire, and that says, "Woman,
there's only tomorrow night, and then
you'll be mine!" And away it flew.

# WELL, SHE FELT THAT HORRID.

However, she heard the king coming along
the passage. In he came, and when he sees
the five skeins, he says, says he, "Well,
my dear," says he, "I don't see but what
you'll have your skeins ready tomorrow
night as well, and as I reckon I shan't
have to kill you, I'll have supper in here
tonight." So they brought supper, and an-
other stool for him, and down the two sate.

# WELL, WHEN HER HUSBAND CAME IN,

there were the five skeins ready for him.

"I see I shan't have to kill you tonight,

my dear," says he. "You'll have your food

and your flax in the morning," says he,

and away he goes.

Well, every day the flax

and the food were brought,

and every day that there little black impet

used to come mornings and evenings.

And all the day the girl sate

trying to think of names to say to it

when it came at night.

But she never hit on the right one.

And as it got towards the end of the month,

the impet began to look so maliceful,

and that twirled that's tail faster and

faster each time she gave a guess.

# WELL, COME THE EVENING

a knocking came again to the window.

She upped and she oped it,

and there was the little old thing

with five skeins of flax on his arm.

"Here it be," says he,

and he gave it to her.

"Now, what's my name?" says he.

"What, is that Bill?" says she.

"Noo, that ain't," says he,

and he twirled his tail.

"Is that Ned?" says she.

"Noo, that ain't," says he,

and he twirled his tail.

"Well, is that Mark?" says she.

"Noo, that ain't," says he,

and he twirled his tail harder, and

away he flew.

**WELL,** the next day,

her husband took her into the room,

and there was the flax and the day's food.

"Now, there's the flax," says he,

"and if that ain't spun up this night,

off goes your head."

And then he went out and locked the door.

He'd hardly gone, when there was a knocking

against the window. She upped and oped it,

and there sure enough was the little old thing

sitting on the ledge.

"Where's the flax?" says he.

"Here it be," says she. And she gave it to him.

"This is what I'll do,"
says the little black thing.
"I'll come to your window every morning
and take the flax and bring it spun at night."
"What's your pay?" says she.

That looked out of the corner of that's eyes,
and that said, "I'll give you three guesses
every night to guess my name, and if you
haven't guessed it before the month's up
you shall be mine."
Well, she thought she'd be sure to guess
that's name before the month was up.
"All right," says she, "I agree."
"All right," that says, and law,

# HOW THAT TWIRLED THAT'S TAIL!

However, all of a sudden
she heard a sort of a knocking
low down on the door.
She upped and oped it,
and what should she see
but a small little black thing
with a long tail.
That looked up at her right curious,
and that said,
"What are you a-crying for?"
"What's that to you?" says she.
"Never you mind," that said,
"but tell me what you're a-crying for."
"That won't do me no good if I do," says she.
"You don't know that," that said,
and twirled that's tail round.
"Well," says she, "that won't do no harm
if that don't do no good,"
and she upped and told about the pies,
and the skeins, and everything.

However, the last day of the eleventh month he takes

her to a room she'd never set eyes on before.

There was nothing in it but a spinning wheel

and a stool. And says he, "Now, my dear,

here you'll be shut in tomorrow with

some victuals and some flax, and if

you haven't spun five skeins by

the night, your head'll go off."

And away he went about

his business.

Well, she was that frightened, she'd

always been such a gatless girl, that she

didn't so much as know how to spin, and what

was she to do tomorrow with no one to come

nigh her to help her? She sat down on the stool and

# LAW, HOW SHE DID CRY!

HE'D WHOLLY FORGOTTEN 'EM.

And for eleven months the girl

had all she liked to eat,

and all the gowns she liked to get,

and all the company she liked to keep.

But when the time was getting over,

she began to think about the skeins

and to wonder if he had 'em in mind.

But not one word did he say about 'em,

AND SHE THOUGHT

Then he said, "Look you here, I want a wife, and I'll marry your daughter. But look you here," says he, "eleven months out of this year she shall have all she likes to eat, and all the gowns she likes to get, and all the company she likes to keep; but the last month of the year she'll have to spin five skeins every day, and if she don't I shall kill her."

"All right," says the woman, for she thought what a grand marriage that was. And as for the five skeins, when the time came, there'd be plenty of ways of getting out of it, and likeliest, he'd have forgotten all about it.

# WELL, SO THEY WERE MARRIED.

The king was coming down the street,

and he heard her sing, but what she sang

he couldn't hear, so he stopped and said,

"What was that you were singing, my good woman?"

The woman was ashamed to let him hear

what her daughter had been doing,

so she sang, instead of that:

MY DARTER HA' SPUN FIVE, FIVE SKEINS TODAY.

MY DARTER HA' SPUN FIVE, FIVE SKEINS TODAY.

# STARS O'MINE! said the king.

"I never heard tell of anyone that could do that."

Well, the woman she was done, and she took her spinning to the door to spin, and as she span she sang:

MY DARTER HA' ATE FIVE, FIVE PIES TODAY.

MY DARTER HA' ATE FIVE, FIVE PIES TODAY.

# WELL, COME SUPPERTIME

the woman said, "Go you, and get one o'
them there pies. I dare say they've come
again now."
The girl went and she looked and there
was nothing but the dishes.

So back she came and says she, "Noo, they
ain't come again."
"Not one of 'em?" says the mother.
"Not one of 'em," says she.
"Well, come again, or not come again,"
said the woman, "I'll have one for supper."
"But you can't, if they ain't come,"
said the girl.
"But I can," says she. "Go you, and bring
the best of 'em."
"Best or worst," says the girl,
"I've ate 'em all, and you can't have one
till that's come again."

# TIME THERE WAS A WOMAN

and she baked five pies. And when they came out of the oven, they were that over-baked the crusts were too hard to eat. So she says to her daughter, "Darter," says she, "put you them there pies on the shelf, and leave 'em there a little, and they'll come again." She meant, you know, the crust would get soft.

But the girl, she says to herself, "Well, if they'll come again, I'll eat 'em now." And she set to work and ate 'em all, first and last.

ONCE UPON A

**To Arni**

Printed in the United States of America
Library of Congress Catalog Card Number 65-14769

"Tom Tit Tot," selected and edited by Joseph Jacobs in
*English Folk and Fairy Tales*, New York: G. P. Putnam's Sons.

# TOM TIT TOT

AN ENGLISH FOLK TALE ILLUSTRATED BY EVALINE NESS

**Charles Scribner's Sons   New York**

# TOM TIT TOT